ANIMAL DETECTIVES

BEE DETECTIVES

Rosie Albright

PowerKiDS press.
New York

Published in 2012 by The Rosen Publishing Group, Inc.
29 East 21st Street, New York, NY 10010

First Edition

Editor: Joanne Randolph
Book Design: Kate Laczynski

Photo Credits: Cover, pp. 5, 6, 8–9, 22–23 Shutterstock.com; pp. 10, 17 Joe Raedle/Getty Images; p. 13 Getty Images News/Getty Images; p. 14 © www.iStockphoto.com/Russ Merritt; p. 18 © Ezra Millstein/The New York Times/Redux; p. 21 DC Photo/Getty Images.

Library of Congress Cataloging-in-Publication Data

Albright, Rosie.
Bee detectives / by Rosie Albright. — 1st ed.
p. cm. — (Animal detectives)
Includes index.
ISBN 978-1-4488-6150-7 (library binding) — ISBN 978-1-4488-6260-3 (pbk.) —
ISBN 978-1-4488-6261-0 (6-pack)
1. Honeybee—Juvenile literature. I. Title.
SF523.5.A53 2012
638′.1—dc23
2011027095

Manufactured in the United States of America

CPSIA Compliance Information: Batch #WW12PK: For Further Information contact Rosen Publishing, New York, New York at 1-800-237-9932

CONTENTS

This is a honeybee. Honeybees drink sweet juice from flowers.

A honeybee finds flowers using its senses. It uses its senses of sight and smell.

A bee uses its **antennae** to smell. Antennae are the sticklike feelers on its head.

RESTRICTED ADMITTANCE
HONEYBEE RESEARCH AREA
CONTACT: Susan Bender 845-9436 or
Phil Rodacy 844-1665

Bees can be trained to find things other than flowers. They have been trained to look for **land mines**.

Beekeepers train bees to find mines. Land mines are used in wars to hurt people.

Land mines are put in the ground. Then they blow up when something touches them.

Bees do not weigh much. They can find the mines without being hurt.

STEEL MINE DETECTION
NUCLEAR DETECTION

Bees can also be used to find **bedbugs**. Bedbugs feed on people's blood.

Bedbugs can live on people's beds. They bite people while they sleep.

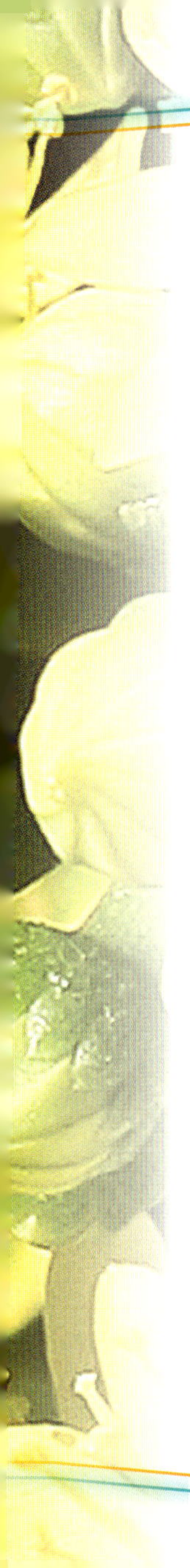

Bees have always helped plants grow. Now bees can help people find land mines and bedbugs.

WORDS TO KNOW

antennae

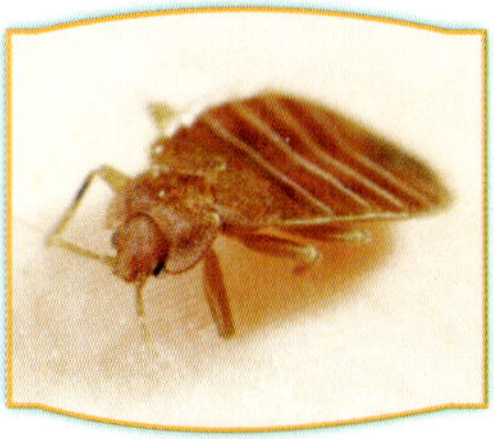
bedbug

land mine

INDEX

WEB SITES

Due to the changing nature of Internet links, PowerKids Press has developed an online list of Web sites related to the subject of this book. This site is updated regularly. Please use this link to access the list: www.powerkidslinks.com/andt/bee/